JIM SMITH
The Frog Band and Durrington Dormouse

LITTLE, BROWN AND COMPANY, BOSTON

Text and illustrations © 1977 by Jim Smith
Library of Congress Catalogue Card No. 77-9187
First American Edition
Publication Code No. T 03-78
ISBN 0-316-80155-0
Printed in Great Britain by William Clowes & Sons, Limited, London, Beccles and Colchester

One hot cloudy July evening many many years ago, Durrington Dormouse, who had recently returned home after a life at sea, decided to spend the evening at the Grasshopper Inn. He snuffed the candles, locked the door, and, sensing it would soon rain again, was quickly on his way.

Just as Durrington was beginning to enjoy the companionship at the Inn, the door burst open and in from the rain rushed a gang of sailors led by a huge bulldog. "Hello, my hearties! Who's for the King's Navy?"

When Durrington heard these words he knew the sailors were a Press Gang who kidnapped innocent victims and forced them to serve in the Navy. Durrington had no wish to go to sea again, so he ran down the cellar stairs, grabbed a gun that was hanging on the wall, and hid behind a barrel!

The bulldog came down the stairs after him with a lantern and searched the cellar, muttering to himself as he failed to discover the missing dormouse. Durrington thought the way was clear and tried to make his escape out of the cellar, but the bulldog saw him, and gave chase!

After what seemed hours, Durrington stopped running and listened. He could no longer hear any sounds of pursuit behind him. By now the storm had worsened. Thunder and lightning filled the skies. "I had better find some shelter till morning," he panted.

During a flash of lightning he spied a dark opening between some bushes, and crawling in, he found himself in a cave. It was very dark, but at least it was dry. Durrington almost jumped out of his fur when a croaky voice close to him said,

"All right, my son, 'tis only me, Mad Maud the Toad. I'll not harm ye.
You look tired, have a drink of this."
By the light of her candle he saw a warty hand holding out a pewter mug
bubbling over with hot liquid.
"Go on, drink it up. It'll give you a good night's rest."

BOOM! BOOM! BOOM!

"What *is* that noise?" said Durrington as he slowly came awake. Daylight glimmered through an opening. "It's time to make a move! That old gal was right, I did have a good sleep. Shiver my timbers, I'm a might stiff this morning!"

Slowly and painfully he squeezed himself out of an old hollow tree. With one last push he tumbled out at the feet of a cheerful frog banging a drum. BOOM! BOOM!

"Hello, old chap! Where did you spring from?" asked the frog as Durrington struggled to his feet. Durrington looked at the crowd of curiously-dressed frogs staring at him. Realising he still had his gun, which was now strangely rusty, he waved it in the air.

"One move and I'll blow you all to Kingdom Come!" he warned.
The frogs dropped their instruments and looked at the dormouse in surprise.
Johann S. Frog gave a little cough and spoke first.
"Ahem! May I introduce myself and my companions? We are the famous Frog
Band, and I am the leader, Johann S. Frog! Surely you must have heard of us?"
"Never heard of ye. As long as you have nothing to do with the Press Gang
last night."

"Last night? What are you talking about!" said the bewildered Johann. "We only arrived here this morning and I'm giving the lads a practice before our concert tomorrow."

Durrington was very puzzled. His best suit had lost all its buttons and was full of holes. And who were these strange looking frogs? Was he dreaming?

"I don't know anything about a concert, but something very peculiar is going on around here and I'd like to know what it is."

He looked again at the frogs. They seemed harmless enough, and the smell of soup cooking made Durrington realise how hungry he was.

"All right lads, relax, – but no tricks! I'm so hungry, I feel as though I haven't eaten for a hundred years!"

Shortie Frog brought him a bowl of delicious soup and some bread, and when Durrington had finished every morsel, he began to tell the frogs of his adventures.

"Press Gangs?" asked Johann.

"There haven't been Press Gangs for over a hundred years!"

Durrington was very upset at this, as he had no idea what Johann was talking about. All he wanted to do was to get back home. Johann ordered the frogs to load their instruments on to their lorry and take Durrington home. Durrington told them the name of his village, and Godfrey Frog found it on the map. He enjoyed the journey, remarking on all the odd things he noticed. He was fascinated by the long poles with strings attached!

There were certainly changes in his village, but the Church and the Grasshopper
Inn seemed much the same. His home was round the corner. There it was, the
same as he had left it, apart from the crowd of animals in the garden, the piles
of furniture on the lawn and the strange carts outside the cottage.

Squire Fox, standing with his friend, Legal Eagle, was very pleased that the eviction of the Dormouse family was going so well. "No trouble at all." The weasels and rats were just bringing out the last of the furniture and putting it in the garden. Soon the cottage would be ready for his nephew to move into. "Hold hard, me hearties! What's going on here?" demanded Durrington as he dashed up to Squire Fox and pushed his gun into Fox's ribs. "Who are you, sir, and this mangy crew? What are you doing in my garden?"

"Put that gun down this instant, you silly old mouse, or I'll get Constable Badger to deal with you," ordered Squire Fox.
Mrs Dormouse tearfully said "Oh, sir, please help us. This wicked Fox is turning us out of our home because he says we are behind with the rent."
"His rent? His house! I'll show him whose house this is!" cried Durrington as he dodged round a removal-rat and darted into the cottage.

Moments later he appeared, covered in soot, and holding a black box.
"Just you look 'ere, my fine fellow!" Durrington shouted and, opening the box,
he waved a yellow piece of parchment at Squire Fox.
"Here it is! All ship shape and Bristol fashion! 'This house belongs to
Durrington Dormouse' – that's me – 'or my heirs.' So what do you think of that,
Mr. Clever Fox?"

Legal Eagle shuffled some papers and said "I say, I say," but Squire Fox made a grab at the box. Snatching it from Durrington, he rushed down the path, shouting to Legal Eagle to follow him. He leapt into his car, and with a grinding of gears he was off! Legal Eagle just managed to flap into the dickie seat as they tore down the road in a cloud of dust.

Durrington and the Frog Band, with Mrs. Dormouse and the other animals, stood with open mouths, too surprised to move. Johann was the first to recover. "Come on, lads, after them!" Durrington and the frogs dashed to the lorry, and Shortie cranked the starting handle. In a cloud of smoke the lorry set off with the angry frogs and Durrington, shouting "Quickly, catch them! My life's savings are in the box!"

Slowly the lorry began to close the gap on Squire Fox. "Oh NO!" the Squire yelled as he saw the level crossing gates ahead about to be closed! But at the sight of the car bearing down on him, the crossing keeper leapt out of the way, leaving just enough room between the gates for Squire Fox to squeeze his car through.

"That will fix them!" said the Squire gleefully, as he looked over his shoulder to see the lorry held up by the closed gates. No sooner were the words spoken when there was an enormous splash as he drove the car straight into the river! With a hiss of steam, the car came to a halt right in the middle, and with a loud crash the dickie seat collapsed on Legal Eagle. By now the crossing gates had opened, and to his horror, Squire Fox saw the Frog Band and Durrington approaching fast. Leaving his trapped friend, the Squire made his rapid escape across the river.

The others drew up and tumbled out of the lorry. "After him, lads!" yelled Durrington at the sight of Squire Fox scrambling up the far bank, "Look for my box!" and to his relief, a Frog found the precious box still in the Squire's abandoned car.

Durrington called off the search for Squire Fox when the sky began to darken. He and Johann, and the Frog Band, and even Legal Eagle, trooped back to a delighted Mrs. Dormouse, who gave a party to celebrate.

Meanwhile, poor Squire Fox was exhausted. He had run until he could no longer hear the sounds of the frogs behind him. It was becoming very dark, and lightning was flickering around him. "I had better find some shelter," he thought. Large drops of rain began to fall. Looking around him, he saw a dark opening between some bushes, and he crawled inside.

It was very dark and still in the cave. He nearly jumped out of his fox fur when a croaky voice said in his ear,

"All right, my son, 'tis only me, Mad Maud the Toad. I'll not harm ye. You look tired, have a drink of this. It'll give you a good night's rest."

He saw by the light of her candle, an old toad lady, holding out to him a pewter mug. Frightened, he drank the bubbling liquid . . .